For Guus

First published in Belgium and Holland by Clavis Uitgeverij, Hasselt – Amsterdam, 2015
Copyright © 2015, Clavis Uitgeverij

English translation from the Dutch by Clavis Publishing Inc. New York
Copyright © 2016 for the English language edition: Clavis Publishing Inc. New York

Visit us on the web at www.clavisbooks.com

Me and My House written and illustrated by Liesbet Slegers
Original title: *Ik en mijn huis*
Translated from the Dutch by Clavis Publishing

ISBN 978-1-60537-250-1

This book was printed in December 2015 at Wai Man Book Binding (China) Ltd. Flat A, 9/F.,
Phase 1, Kwun Tong Industrial Centre, 472-484 Kwun Tong Road, Kwun Tong, Kowloon, H.K.

First Edition
10 9 8 7 6 5 4 3 2 1

Me
and My House

Liesbet Slegers

Clavis

NEW YORK

My house

My things

Here is my **closet**.
My clothes are in my closet.
Here are my shorts and one of my socks!

Here are **Bear**, **Dog**, and **Blankie**.
I ride my bike and they come along with me.
There we go!

Here is my **stool**, and here is my **chair**.
I sit on the stool.
Bear can sit in the big chair today!

Here are my **bib**, my **bowl**,
my **cup**, and my **spoon**.
I use my spoon to eat from my bowl.
Yummy, that's good!

Here are my **blocks**, my **plane** and my **doll**.
My doll climbs on the tower of blocks and my plane flies through the air!

Here are my **washcloth**, my **ducky** and my **soap**.
Mommy puts soap on the washcloth.
First she washes me, and then I wash my ducky.

Here are my **books**.
I look at them all.
I see a sun and a tree.
And look, a little bird!

Here are my **blankie**, my **bed**
and my **night-light**.
My night-light stays on all night.
Sleep tight!

Sounds

Ring, ring! Here is the **telephone**.
Oh, it's Grandma on the line!
How are you, Grandma?

Voo-oom! Here is the **vacuum cleaner**.
Mommy is cleaning.
The vacuum cleaner makes so much noise!

VOO-OOM

Hi everyone! Here is the tv.
Look who's here — two friends!
I watch my favorite shows.

Tralala! Here is the **radio**.
Someone is singing a beautiful song.
I sing along!

Tick, tock! Here is the **clock**.
The clock hangs on the wall
and tells the time.

Woo-oo! Here is the **hair dryer.**
Mommy dries her hair
and I brush my hair until it shines.

Rrrr-rrrr! Here is the **washing machine.**
My dirty clothes are inside.
They spin around and get clean.

Whoosh! Here is the **toilet**.
I flush.
Wow, there's so much water!

Things in
the house

Here is a plant.
It's on a windowsill in the sun.
That's why it grows so well.

Here is the **light**.
I press the switch.
Light on! Light off!

Here is the **comfy chair**
with a **pillow**.
It is my favorite chair.
I can read a book here.

Here is the **table**, and here are the **chairs**.
I can sit on the chairs,
but I also drive my cars on them. Vroom!

Here is the **cupboard**.
The doors can open and close.
There are all sorts of things in the cupboard.

Here is Daddy's **computer**.
Sometimes he lets me use it too.
I touch the keys very carefully.

Here is the **mirror**.
Look, that's me. Isn't it funny?
I wave at myself.

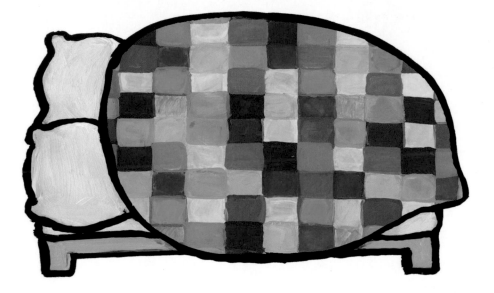

Here is Mommy and Daddy's **big bed.**
They go to sleep under the cozy blankets.
Sweet dreams!